terrible
things

ordinary
terrible
things

I made this book for kids who grow up in a culture that is obsessed with sex and obsessed with hiding it from them, and who want to know what the big deal is.

Too often, kids learn that sex is outside of them, something that "happens" in puberty, in love, or in marriage. Too often, sex is presented as a "threat"—of pregnancy, disease, abandonment, and violence. Too often, kids learn about sex from porn.

But we could give children permission to awaken to their own sexual energy from its very first flutter, and study that instead. We could offer sex education for boys that's no different than what we offer girls and includes all who are between and beyond girl and boy, who demand better words—*intersex, transgender, gender-nonconforming*—words that can change and evolve and that everyone can learn, if they try.

Every child deserves a place where it's safe to talk about danger, where they can ask any question in an atmosphere of love and ease, and where they can get answers that do no harm, but see and embrace them as they are. When I think of that wise, safe, accepting authority, I see a grandma like the one in this book.

Many of us did not have a grandmother we could talk to about sex. But I can imagine a world where old women command the utmost respect, where even young children are entrusted with the knowledge of and authority over their own bodies and power. That is the world I want to be part of shaping.

With love and trust,

Anastasia

TELL ME ABOUT SEX, GRANDMA

Written and Illustrated by Anastasia Higginbotham

dottir press

new york city

Published in 2021 by Dottir Press
33 Fifth Avenue
New York, NY 10003

dottirpress.com

SECOND EDITION

Illustration and text by Anastasia Higginbotham
Photography by Alexa Hoyer
Production and design by Drew Stevens
Additional art by Sabatino Luongo Higginbotham

Special thanks to Sabatino Luongo Higginbotham for painting rainbows, cutting oranges, and
inspiring this sparkling child.

Distributed to the trade by Consortium Book Sales and Distribution, www.cbsd.com.

Contact Jennifer Baumgardner at jb@dottirpress.com for any questions about bulk purchases,
classroom use, book donations, or collaborations.

Library of Congress Cataloging-in-Publication Data is available for this title.
ISBN 978-1-9483-4042-7
eISBN 978-1-9483-4047-2

for
gono

who Knows what
sex is and
what it isn't,

and

for Susan and Sharon,
who are healers.

4

Sex is everywhere.

Knowing where to look ...

when
you want
to find
answers ...

...is Key.

15

Curiosity about sex
is your birthright.

click!

It's in your nature
to want to Know...

Well,
whattaya
wanna
Know?

19

...where you came from,
what you're made of,
what sex is,
        and

...what it isn't.

I'm not supposed to see it, know it, or do it — like a swear or a secret. So it must be bad.

Sex is already part of you.
You were born with it.

28

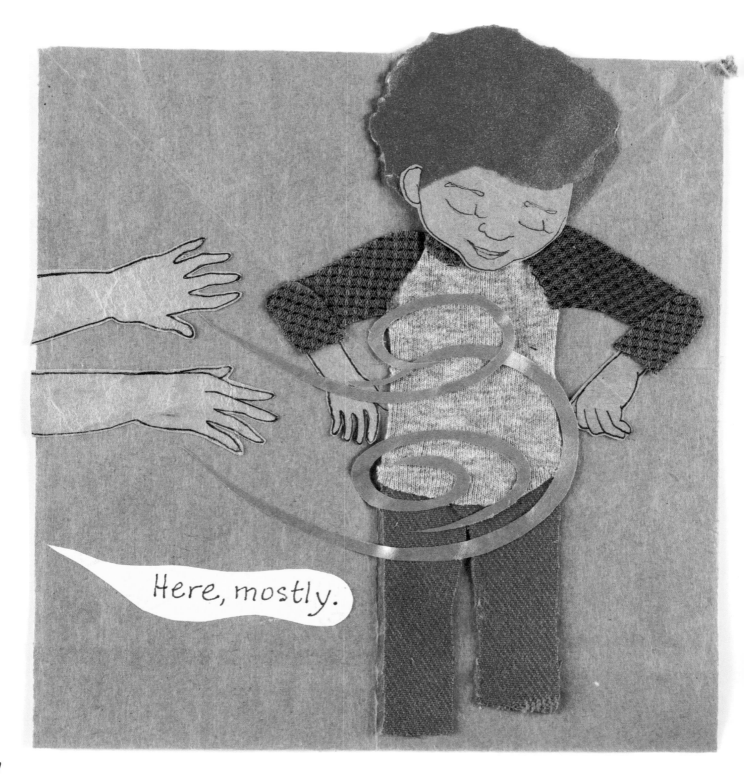

34

The feelings change as
you grow up.

They grow up
with you.

Sex is an energy, an action,
a conversation,
a revelation.*

* Sudden burst of
understanding
or discovery.

Your sexuality is
something you discover
as you go along —

how you feel,
what you like,

and who you like.

43

to boss you into sex, or

take it from you without your permission.

You get to choose
whether to
do it.

47

And from people who don't follow the rules.

It is never okay
for an adult to choose
to have sex with a child
—— even if they
love and take care
of you.

What rules?

Your sexuality
is yours alone.

Yours to discover.
Yours to treasure.

May your choices about sex always be yours to make....

What does your dolphin say to you?

"She says, "Thank you for my ocean.""

... whether or not you ever decide to do it.

The end.

Read this next part out loud:

I am the one-and-only, top-boss, in-charge decider about sex in my life for my whole life. Everyone else is the boss of themself too.

When there's a choice to make
— any choice at all —
it helps to know what you
want.

Do you get a feeling of

YES NO

L
O
O
K

here →

stop
go

SLOW ZONE

about any of these images? ⟶

You are already making choices all the time about what you like and...

...what you want. You know a lot.

Sex is POWERFUL. So are you.

Be aware: There is an abyss* of images out there that can distort and even ruin your experience of learning about sex.

*bottomless pit

Those aren't the answers you're looking for. Move along.

Choose a grown-up who will help you answer your questions safely.

In the meantime and for all time...

Be safe.
Be you.
Be loved.

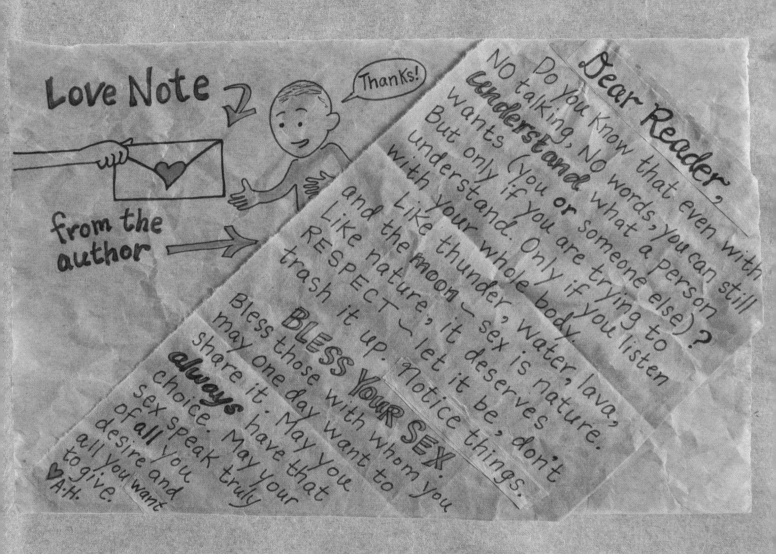

ordinary terrible things

ordinary terrible things